The Simple People

by Tedd Arnold · pictures by Andrew Shachat

Dial Books for Young Readers New York

Teach us delight in simple things,
And mirth that has no bitter springs;
Forgiveness free of evil done,
And love to all men 'neath the sun!
Rudyard Kipling

To mothers and fathers
–Tedd Arnold

To people all over the world working to protect the earth
–Andrew Shachat

Published by Dial Books for Young Readers
A Division of Penguin Books USA Inc.
375 Hudson Street • New York, New York 10014

Text copyright © 1992 by Tedd Arnold
Illustrations copyright © 1992 by Andrew Shachat
Printed in Hong Kong by South China Printing Company (1988) Limited
First Edition
1 3 5 7 9 10 8 6 4 2

Library of Congress Cataloging in Publication Data
Arnold, Tedd.
The simple people / by Tedd Arnold; illustrated by Andrew Shachat.
p. cm.
Summary: The simple people enjoy the simple life, until Node's
craftwork is used to make life complicated, and everyone forgets the
feel of the sun and the taste of fresh fruit.
ISBN 0-8037-1012-7 (trade).—ISBN 0-8037-1013-5 (library)
[1. Simplicity—Fiction.] I. Shachat, Andrew, ill. II. Title.
PZ7.A7379Sj 1992 [E]—dc20 91-17697 CIP AC

The full-color artwork was prepared with inks, watercolors,
colored pencils, and acrylic paint. It was then color-separated
and reproduced in red, blue, yellow, and black halftones.

The simple people lived under trees beside a clear blue spring.
They sang songs and ate sweet fruit. The days were warm, the wind
was soft, and life was simple.

Sometimes Node made simple things with sticks and vines. He would hang the things in trees. The wind would blow through them saying, *"Oh-h-h-h-h."*

One day Node was looking through something he had made, when
Bog came up and asked, "What is that?"

"It's just something to look through," answered Node.

Bog took it. "That's nice," he said, "but do you expect me to hold
it up the entire time I'm looking?" Node didn't expect anything of
the sort. He was simply going to hang it from a tree.

"What you need," said Bog, "are more sticks to hold it up."

"More sticks?" said Node.

"More sticks!" said Bog.

They both looked through the look-through thing held up by sticks. Pug walked over and watched them.

"Those sticks are shaky and weak," said Pug. "These rocks will hold it steady and strong."

Node didn't think it needed rocks or sticks. But Bog spoke up.
"You're right, Pug. And more rocks will make it even stronger."
"More rocks?" said Pug.
"More rocks!" said Bog.

Other people began gathering rocks too. They sang as they worked.
Soon everyone was gathering rocks. Everyone but Node.

He didn't think they needed more rocks. He stood by his look-through and watched as the rock pile grew higher and longer.

"It's a wall!" declared Bog.

No one had seen a wall before. The people were so pleased with it that they kept adding to it. Day after day the wall grew.

One day Node noticed the people no longer sang as they worked. They were too tired.

But they didn't stop. Bog had each of them doing a special job.

Some were rock diggers.

Some were rock carriers.

Others were rock stackers.

If one person stopped, others would have to wait. Then the work would not get done. So Bog gave some people the job of making sure everybody else did their jobs. Node thought it was getting very complicated.

Eventually the wall became too long to carry rocks from one end to the other. So they curved it around in a big circle. One day the ends met and the wall surrounded them.

Pug asked Bog, "What shall we do now?"
"We have plenty of room to build more walls," answered Bog.

"More walls?" said Pug.
"More walls!" said Bog.

Everyone began building walls inside the circular wall. Everyone but Node. He didn't think they needed more walls. He stood by his look-through and listened to the wind whisper, *"Oh-h-h-h-h."*

Soon there was no room to build more inside walls.

Pug asked Bog, "What shall we do now?"

Bog took a fruit tree and began building a roof. "We will need many more trees," he said.

"More trees?" said Pug.

"More trees!" said Bog.

It became dark inside the walls as everyone helped build the roof. Everyone but Node. He didn't think they needed a roof. He stood by his look-through and enjoyed the only bit of sunlight there was inside the wall.

When the roof was finished, Pug asked Bog, "What now?"

Bog went to the clear blue spring, made a batch of mud, and spread it on the rough rock wall. "We can make smooth walls," he said, "if we mix up a lot more mud."

"More mud?" asked Pug.

"More mud!" answered Bog.

It was so dark that people built fires to see by as they made mud. Everyone helped spread the mud on the walls and ceiling. Everyone but Node. He didn't think the walls needed to be smooth. He didn't think the walls needed to be there at all.

One day Node was hungry and wandered away from his look-through. The walls made many bends and turns. Node asked where he could find some fruit, but everyone was too busy to answer him.

Meanwhile Pug found the sunny opening in the wall. He carefully patched it and smoothed it over because that was his job. He went away looking for more places to patch.

Node searched, but he found no fruit. His eyes began to hurt, and he grew dizzy breathing smoke from all the fires. He decided to return to his look-through for some fresh air. He walked and walked, but he couldn't find it.

After hours of searching, he bumped into Pug who was patching a little crack.

"Pug, have you seen my look-through?" he asked.

"I don't remember," Pug answered. "I haven't been feeling too well." He began to cough.

Node went on searching, never knowing when it was day or night. He stumbled down one dark passageway after another. The people he passed were sick, and no one was working. All he could find to eat and drink was bitter moss growing on the walls and muddy water where the clear blue spring once flowed.

He could barely remember the last time he had tasted sweet fruit or sang a song or played in the sunlight.

At last, too tired to walk any farther, Node leaned against a smooth wall to rest.

He heard a whisper and looked around, but no one was there. It sounded familiar, but Node couldn't remember why.

He looked at the wall and saw a tiny white crack.

Putting his ear to the crack, he could hear the whisper clearly. *"Oh-h-h-h-h."*

Suddenly he remembered the wind and fresh air and sunlight.

He took a rock and chipped away at the crack. A thin patch of mud covered the look-through he had made so long ago.

As he chipped all the mud away, sunlight and wind rushed into the darkness.

Node climbed out. He breathed fresh air and danced in the light.

After a moment he climbed back inside. One by one he helped other people find the opening. They all climbed out.

Everyone feasted on sweet fruits and sang happily for the first time since the wall had been started.

The night was warm, the wind was soft,
and life was simple once more.